OH BEANS!
St★rring Snap Bean

BEANS
ONLY

BY ELLEN WEISS • ILLUSTRATED BY SUSAN T. HALL

Troll Associates

"Put it over there, not over here!"
"Don't drop that, you bean-brain!"
"How can you be so clumsy!"
The beans were building a new clubhouse, and Snap Bean was yelling at everyone.

"Why don't you ever think before you do things?" he snapped at Half-Baked Bean.

"Stay out from underfoot!" he snapped at Bean Sprout.

"Don't just sit there," he snapped at Lima Bean. "Hurry up! Get to work!"

"Snap Bean," said Vanilla Bean sweetly, "could you yell just a teensy bit less? It would make things a lot more fun for us."

"Stop being so nice all the time!" snapped Snap Bean. "It really gets on my nerves!"

Soon it was time to put on the roof.

"Let's all lift it together," suggested Vanilla Bean.

"Okay, everybeany," said Lima Bean. "A-one, and a-two, and a—"

"Wait a second!" cried Half-Baked Bean. "I don't have a good grip on it!"

"You dodo-bean!" snapped Snap Bean. "Can't you do anything right?"

"That does it," said Half-Baked Bean in a huff. "I'm not getting snapped at any more. I'm going home." And off he went.

But Snap Bean kept right on snapping. "Look at this place! It's all a big mess, because nobody's listening to *me!*"

"Okay, everybeany, let's try it again," said Lima Bean with a sigh. "A-one, and a-two, and a—"

Up went the roof! But the roof looked very strange.

"This roof is crooked!" Snap Bean snapped. "Bean Sprout, it's all your fault. You're just too little to get the job done right!"

Little Bean Sprout began to cry.

"Oh, beans!" said Vanilla Bean. "That's not true! Bean Sprout is doing her best. Besides, you should be ashamed of yourself, snapping at a little bean. Come on, Bean Sprout. I'm taking you home. I guess we're not wanted here."

And off they went together.

"If you had listened to me, you'd have done things right!" Snap Bean yelled after them.

Snap Bean screamed and stamped his feet. He was mad enough to go right through the roof.

And that's just what Snap Bean did.

The roof and the walls came tumbling down. "Whew!" he said, blinking his eyes. "Now we can start all over again, doing it *my* way, of course!"

He looked around, waiting for someone to agree. But nobody answered. They had all gone home. There was no one left to snap at.

"And no one to bother me," thought Snap Bean. "Now I can do it myself."

First he tried putting up the front wall. But the front wall wouldn't stay up. "Stupid, dumb wall," Snap Bean snapped as the front wall fell on his foot.

Then he tried putting up the back wall. But the back wall wouldn't stay up.

"You're even dumber than the front wall!" he screamed as the back wall hit his head.

Suddenly, Snap Bean heard a voice.

"Need some help?" Vanilla Bean asked. "Maybe if you'd try not to lose your temper, we could all get the job done together."

Snap Bean had to admit she was right. Getting mad hadn't helped things at all.

Slowly and carefully, he picked up the back wall and started to put it in place. It began to wobble. It almost fell down.

Then he felt two strong hands beside his.

"I thought you could use some help," said Lima Bean.

"Maybe I *could,*" Snap Bean admitted.

The clubhouse began to take shape again as everyone got back to work.

Snap Bean tried very hard to stay calm, even when something went wrong.

"I will not snap," he told himself. "I will not snap at all."

The beans worked together until all that was left was to put the chimney in place.

But Lima Bean knocked over the chimney.

"Lima Bean!" Snap Bean started to snap. "Lima Bean, you are soooo . . . helpful!"

Lima Bean smiled as he put the chimney back up.

The clubhouse was finished at last!

"Wow," Snap Bean said as he looked at the clubhouse. "I could never have done that alone."

Snap Bean turned to Vanilla Bean and smiled. "You were right. When I'm not bean snappy, we're *all* a lot more happy. And working *together* really gets the job done."